The Pony-Mad Princess

Princess Ellie
to the
Rescue

"Well done," said Meg as
Sundance walked forward again.

Ellie glowed with pride. Then
she looked back at the woods.
The face had gone. Perhaps she
had imagined it. But as they rode
away, she had the strangest feeling
she was being watched.

Look out for more sparkly adventures of
The Pony-Mad Princess!

The Pony-Mad Princess

Princess Ellie
to the
Rescue

Diana Kimpton

Illustrated by Lizzie Finlay

USBORNE

For Jasmine

This edition first published in 2014 by Usborne Publishing Ltd.,
Usborne House, 83-85 Saffron Hill, London EC1N 8RT, England.
www.usborne.com

First published in 2004. Based on an original concept by Anne Finnis.
Text copyright © 2004 by Diana Kimpton and Anne Finnis.

Illustrations copyright © 2004 by Lizzie Finlay.

A CIP catalogue record for this book is available from the British Library.

ISBN 9781409565963   JFMA JJASOND/14 01423/6

Printed in Chatham, Kent, UK.

Chapter 1

"Bother," said the Princess as the book she'd been balancing on her head crashed to the floor.

Miss Stringle picked it up and sighed as she looked at the title. "Not again, Princess Aurelia. Perhaps you would find waving lessons easier if you practised more instead of reading these silly pony stories."

"But I like them. And I like to be called Princess *Ellie*."

Miss Stringle sighed again. "I've told you before. That is not a suitable name for a princess." She held out the book. "Now, stand as tall as you can and try once more."

Ellie straightened her head, balanced the book carefully on top of it and set out across the room. The skirt of her frothy pink dress swirled around her legs as she walked.

"No, no!" shouted Miss Stringle. "Dainty steps. Not big strides."

Ellie slowed down.

"Now wave," said Miss Stringle.

Ellie raised her right hand slowly and waved at an imaginary crowd.

"And smile!"

Princess Ellie to the Rescue

Ellie pulled her lips back and showed her teeth. She didn't feel like smiling. She felt very foolish. No one in her pony books ever had to do anything like this. They had masses of friends, went to ordinary schools and spent all their spare time having fun with their ponies. All the things that Ellie wanted, but couldn't have. Sometimes Ellie hated being a princess.

She reached the other side of the room with relief and let the book slide off her head. "I've finished," she said, as she caught it neatly. "Can I go now?"

Miss Stringle smiled. "Of course you can, Your Highness. Have a lovely ride."

Ellie raced out of the palace classroom and up the spiral staircase to her bedroom. It was probably the pinkest room in the entire world. Her father, the King, had planned the decorations when she was born and he was convinced princesses liked pink.

Ellie didn't. She had managed to cover the pink walls with pony posters and bookcases full of pony books. But there was nothing she could do about the rose pink carpet, pink striped curtains and pink four-poster bed.

Princess Ellie to the Rescue

She threw off her dress
and grabbed her pale pink
jodhpurs from a cupboard.
As she struggled into them,
she glanced at the clock. She
didn't want to be late. George
was always cross when she
was late.

Then she remembered.
George wasn't there any more. After caring
for the royal horses for forty years, he had
retired to the seaside. Today she would
meet the new groom for the first time.

She pulled on her shiny
black leather riding boots,
thankful that no one in
the kingdom made
pink ones her size.

"It will be strange without George," she thought. "I wonder if the new groom will have as many rules." George had hundreds of them, most of which began, "Princesses don't..."

Ellie pushed her everyday crown on her head and picked up her hard hat. She paused for a moment to straighten its gold and pink silk cover. Then she ran out of the room and down the back staircase to the stables.

To her surprise, there was no sign of the new groom. But there was a new horse. A beautiful grey thoroughbred looked out of the stable where George's horse had lived. She walked over to him and stroked his neck. His coat was as soft as velvet. The horse whickered gently and nuzzled her pockets in search of titbits.

Princess Ellie to the Rescue

"Hello."

The cheerful voice made Ellie jump. She turned and saw a tall, slim woman walking towards her carrying a saddle and bridle. She had friendly brown eyes and her long, dark hair was tied back in a ponytail.

"I see you've met my Gipsy," said the woman as she put the saddle on the stable door. "I'm Meg. I'm the new groom. And you, I imagine, are Princess Aurelia."

Ellie nodded nervously.

"That's a real mouthful of a name," continued Meg with a smile. "Are you always called that or do your friends shorten it?"

"I like to be called Ellie," she replied, bravely. She didn't mention that she hadn't any friends or that everyone else insisted on calling her Aurelia or "Your Royal Highness".

"All right then. Ellie it is." Meg grinned and pulled a sheet of royal notepaper from her pocket. "This note from your father says you want to ride Sundance today."

"Yes, please," said Ellie, hardly able to believe what she'd just heard. Meg was the first person to ever call her Ellie. Maybe everything would be different now. Maybe she could have as much fun with her ponies as the children did in her books.

"Then you'd better get him tacked up.
I'll see to Gipsy and then we can be off."

Meg went into Gipsy's stable leaving Ellie
open-mouthed with shock. George had
never let her do anything in the stables.
Although she had four ponies of her own,
she had never been allowed to look after
them. She knew tacking up meant putting
on the saddle and bridle. But she had
absolutely no idea how to do it.

Chapter 2

For a moment, Ellie wondered if she should ask for help. But this was the first chance she had ever had to do something in the stables by herself. If Meg realized how little she knew, she might not let her try again. "Tacking up can't be that difficult," she thought. "I'm sure I can work out how to do it."

Princess Ellie to the Rescue

Ellie walked over to the tack room and hesitated. This had been George's special place. She could almost hear him saying, "Princesses don't go in there." But George wasn't around any more and Meg had told her to fetch Sundance's saddle. It must be all right to go in.

Ellie stepped inside and breathed in the lovely smell of leather. The saddles were on racks along one wall with the bridles hanging underneath. She stared at them nervously.

They all looked the same. How could she tell which was Sundance's? Then she realized that above each one was a nameplate decorated with a golden crown.

Sundance's rack was so high that she had to stand on tiptoe to reach it. The saddle was heavier than she expected. The bridle wasn't, but it was hard to carry them both at the same time. The reins dragged on the ground as she walked across the yard.

"Hello, Sundance," she said as she went into the stable. The chestnut pony pricked his ears forward in a friendly way and walked towards her. His feet rustled the thick layer of straw on the floor.

"I'm tacking you up today," she told the pony. Her voice sounded more confident than she felt. She carefully put the saddle on the door just as Meg had done with Gipsy's. Then she looked at the bridle. She could recognize the reins and the metal bit which went in Sundance's mouth. But there seemed to be so many other straps and buckles. She wasn't sure which ones she had to undo.

"I'll just have to guess," she decided. She chose one of the buckles and unfastened it. The bit swung down and dangled by one

strap. She had no idea if that was supposed
to happen. So she picked another buckle
and undid that one. The bit fell off completely
and landed in the straw. She was sure that
was wrong.

Sundance seemed
to think so too. He
put his head down
and nuzzled the bit
curiously.

Suddenly the
door swung open and
Meg came in. "How
are you getting on?"
she asked. Then she
saw the pieces
of the bridle
and laughed.

Princess Ellie to the Rescue

Ellie felt so stupid that she nearly burst into tears. But she didn't want Meg to see her cry so she did the only other thing she could think of. She thrust the tangle of straps into Meg's hands, put on her most royal expression and stormed out of the stable saying, "Princesses don't tack up."

Chapter 3

As soon as Ellie was outside she felt even more stupid. She had always wanted to look after her ponies herself, like the children in her books. Now she had spoiled the only chance she ever had to do it.

She sniffed loudly and wiped away a tear with the back of her hand. Then she walked miserably along the yard to Rainbow's stable. The grey Welsh pony was standing quietly with her head over the door. Ellie gave Rainbow a peppermint and stroked her neck. The warm smell of horse made Ellie feel calmer.

She moved along to the next stable and saw Moonbeam, the palomino, quietly eating hay. Her mane and tail were snow white and the rest of her was a beautiful creamy gold. She came over when she saw Ellie and politely took a peppermint from her hand. Then she nuzzled Ellie's pockets looking for more.

Suddenly there was a loud noise from the end stable. Shadow, the black Shetland, had smelled the peppermints and was banging the wall to make sure he wasn't forgotten. Ellie ran along the yard to see him. He was too small to put his head over the door so she had to reach down to give him his sweet. She ruffled his mane and sighed as he crunched it. "I've ruined everything," she said.

Then she heard a clatter of hooves behind her. She turned around and saw Meg leading Sundance.

"I've tacked him up for you," she said, gently. "Do you still want to ride?"

"Yes, please," said Ellie, her voice unsteady from the nearness of her tears. "And I'm sorry I was rude."

"That's all right," said Meg. "It was wrong of me to laugh. I should have checked you knew what to do." She pulled down the stirrups and held Sundance's reins. "Now jump on and we'll have a lovely ride to cheer you up."

Ellie felt better once she was on Sundance's back. She leaned forward and patted the chestnut pony's neck while she watched Meg mount Gipsy. Then she followed her out of the yard and into the palace grounds.

As they rode side by side, Meg asked, "Did you mean what you said in the stable? You don't have to tack up if you don't want to."

"But I do," said Ellie, quickly. "I want to tack up and groom and muck out and

make feeds and clean saddles and
everything." Then she stopped and added
quietly, "But I don't know how. George
never let me."

"Then I'd better teach you," said Meg.
"But first of all, let's have a gallop across this
field. Unless princesses *don't* gallop."

Ellie laughed, happily. "This one does,"
she said.

"Follow me then," said Meg, and raced
away on Gipsy.

Ellie squeezed her legs against
Sundance's sides. The pony leaped forward
willingly and galloped after the grey
thoroughbred. Ellie leaned forward in the
saddle and felt the wind whistle past her
face. She could hear Sundance's hooves
drumming on the ground as the pony
carried her swiftly across the grass.

As they neared the other side of the field,
Sundance started to tire. Ellie let him slow
to a gentle canter until they reached the

fence where Meg was waiting. Then they rode slowly along the edge of the field, letting Sundance and Gipsy get their breath back.

A fox trotted across their path. It stopped for a moment to look at them before continuing calmly on its way. Ellie watched as it squeezed under the fence and disappeared into a patch of woodland. She peered between the trees trying to catch another glimpse of it. But instead she saw a human face looking back at her.

Suddenly a bird flew out from the bushes and startled Sundance. He snorted with fear and jumped sideways. The movement took Ellie by surprise. Her left foot came out of its stirrup and for a moment she thought she was going to fall off. But she managed to

stay in the saddle and soon calmed her
pony down.

"Well done," said Meg as Sundance
walked forward again.

Ellie glowed with pride. Then she looked
back at the woods. The face had gone.
Perhaps she had imagined it. But as they
rode away, she had the strangest feeling
that she was being watched.

Chapter 4

The pleasure of riding soon stopped Ellie wondering any more about the mysterious watcher. By the time they got back to the palace, she had almost forgotten the whole incident. "That's the best ride I've ever had," she told Meg. "I loved that gallop."

"So did I," said Meg. "Now put Sundance in his stable and I'll show you how to look after him."

First, Meg taught Ellie how to run the stirrups up to the top of the leathers and undo the girth so the saddle came off easily. Then, she showed her which strap to undo on the bridle and how to pull it off gently so the bit fell out of Sundance's mouth without banging his teeth. Finally, Meg handed Ellie a brush and told her to brush the saddle mark off the pony's back while she put the saddle and bridle away.

The Pony-Mad Princess

Ellie was blissfully happy. It was warm in the stable and it smelled of horse. For the first time, Sundance really felt like her own pony.

"Is there anything else I can do?" she asked when Meg came back.

"You can help me fill the haynets and water buckets if you like. But don't you have to get back for dinner?"

Ellie knew it was getting late but she was reluctant to leave when she was enjoying herself so much. "I've loads of time," she said, knowing it wasn't quite true. Surely it wouldn't matter if she was late just this once.

Meg took her to the barn and showed her how to fill the nets with armfuls of soft, sweet-smelling hay. "Make sure it's hay, not

straw," she said.
"It's easy to tell
the difference.
The straw
has thicker
stems."

The job took much longer than Ellie had
expected and it was nearly dark by the time
they had finished. Meg went to hang the hay
in the stables while Ellie filled the water
buckets. She had never carried buckets full
of water before and was surprised how heavy
they were. To make matters worse, the water

slopped about as
she walked so her
jodhpurs and
boots were
soon
soaked.

"You really need some wellingtons," said
Meg, when she saw how wet Ellie was. "And
it might be a good idea to leave your crown
at home."

"It's only my everyday one," said Ellie. "Mum
and Dad would be cross if I didn't wear it. But
they might agree to welly boots. I'll ask them
this evening." Then she remembered. This
evening the Prime Minister was coming to

dinner. It was really important she got there on time. She'd be in real trouble if she was late. She glanced at her watch and panicked. "Oh no!" she cried. "I'm late. I've got to go." She dumped the last bucket in Sundance's stable and shut the door. Then she ran off across the yard.

"Thanks for your help," Meg shouted after her. "See you in the morning."

Ellie paused just long enough to wave goodbye before she raced over to the back door of the palace and hurtled up the stairs to her bedroom.

The clock beside her bed stared at her accusingly. Its bright pink hands showed she had only five minutes to get clean, changed, and down to the dining room.

The Pony-Mad Princess

Ellie glanced at herself in the long mirror
on the wall. She didn't look much like a
princess at the moment. Her face was dirty,
her hair was a mess, and her cheeks were
red from excitement and exercise.

"There's no time for a shower," she
thought as she pulled off her jacket and shirt.
"I'll just have to do the best I can." She
washed her hands quickly, wiped the dirty
marks off her face with a wet flannel and
pulled the hay out of her curly, blonde hair
with a comb. Then she popped
her tiara on her head and
slipped on one of her
best dresses. It was a
deep rose pink with
sequins on the bodice
and several layers of net

petticoat under the knee-length skirt. Ellie's fingers struggled with the white satin sash as she tried to tie it in a bow behind her back.

As soon as she had succeeded, she ran down the spiral stairs and along the corridor to the dining room. Her feet were almost silent on the thick red carpet. She paused outside the door, smoothing the folds of her skirt as she tried to calm herself down. Then she stood up as straight as Miss Stringle had taught her, and went in.

The King and Queen were already at the table chatting to the Prime Minister. They all looked up when she arrived. But slowly their smiles changed to looks of surprise. They seemed to be staring at her feet.

Ellie looked down and groaned. Sticking out from the bottom of her dress was a pair of very dirty jodhpurs and an even dirtier pair of boots. She had been in such a rush that she'd forgotten to take them off.

Chapter 5

Ellie wondered desperately what to do. Should she leave or should she stay? Then she made up her mind. She couldn't keep them waiting even longer while she got changed properly. She'd just have to act as if nothing was wrong.

Trying to look more confident than she felt, she strode across to the candle-lit table and sat down in her place. "I'm so sorry to have kept you waiting," she said.

To her relief, the Queen followed Ellie's lead. "Well, at least you're here now," she said, waving to the servants to bring the food.

Ellie was determined not to do anything else wrong. She tried hard to eat her meal in the way Miss Stringle had taught her. She chose the correct silver knife and fork from the gleaming selection by her plate, kept her mouth closed while she chewed, and only spilt a couple of drops of gravy on the crisp, white tablecloth. She even remembered not to drum her feet against the chair leg or play with her crystal glass while the adults talked politics.

At first the smell of wet jodhpurs and horse was hardly noticeable. But the room was very warm and the warmth made the smell grow stronger and stronger. By the time they had finished their strawberries and ice cream, Ellie was sure it was impossible to ignore.

She looked nervously round the table to see if any of the others had noticed. The Prime Minister obviously had. When he realized she was looking at him, he wrinkled his nose and sniffed dramatically.

"How are things at the stables?" he asked with a smile.

"Wonderful," said Ellie. "We've a new groom and she's going to let me look after my ponies myself."

"Really!" said the Queen with surprise. "And what exactly does that involve?"

"It's grooming and mucking out and cleaning tack and filling buckets and…"

"But that's work," said the King. "You're a princess, Aurelia, and princesses don't work."

Ellie stared at him in dismay. What if he wouldn't allow her to look after her ponies? What if he sent Meg away and got another groom like George?

Princess Ellie to the Rescue

"But it's much more fun than sitting in the palace on my own," she said.

"That doesn't make any difference," said the King, firmly.

The Prime Minister coughed gently to attract their attention. "Perhaps it makes it a hobby rather than work," he said and winked at Ellie.

Ellie grinned at him in delight. "That's right," she said, bravely. "It's definitely a hobby. And I'm sure princesses are allowed to have hobbies."

The Queen smiled. "I'm sure they are too," she said. "Provided they remember to get changed before they come to dinner."

Ellie was so delighted that she jumped up and kissed her. "I promise I will," she said. She decided not to mention the wellingtons. It seemed more sensible to stop while she was winning.

Chapter 6

The next morning, Ellie leaped out of bed as soon as she woke up. It was Saturday so there were no lessons. Instead, she could spend the whole day at the stables.

She was already dressed by the time the maid arrived with her breakfast on a silver tray.

Ellie ignored the perfectly boiled egg and gulped down the orange juice. Then she grabbed the buttered toast and ate it as she ran down to the stables.

"I thought you and Sundance might like a lesson today," said Meg. "But first we'll turn the others out into the field."

Ellie chose to lead Shadow. She thought he would be the easiest because he was the smallest. But she was wrong. Rainbow and Moonbeam walked quietly, but Shadow didn't want to. Every few steps he dropped his head to grab a mouthful of grass or dived into the hedge to eat tasty leaves. Soon, Ellie's arm ached from being yanked in one direction after another.

She was relieved when they reached the field. Meg turned Rainbow and Moonbeam loose first. They trotted across the grass together, arching their necks and sniffing the morning air. Ellie watched them go. Then she carefully unbuckled Shadow's headcollar and took it off. But the little Shetland had much less energetic ideas. He didn't go anywhere. He just started eating the grass in front of him.

Back in the yard, Meg helped Ellie to groom Sundance. He seemed to enjoy it and lifted his feet willingly so Ellie could clean them out with a hoof pick.

When his coat was gleaming and his hooves were freshly painted with oil, Meg showed Ellie how to put on his saddle and bridle. Then they set off to the sand school for the lesson. It was a big area of sand with a wooden fence around the outside and some jumps in the middle.

Ellie had ridden in there many times with George but this time she felt very nervous. She was worried in case Meg didn't think her riding was good enough. She tried hard to keep her heels down and her back straight as she trotted Sundance round the school. He wasn't nervous at all. He trotted confidently with his head up and his ears pricked forward. Soon, Ellie relaxed too and started to enjoy herself. Meg was a good teacher and quick to praise everything she did right.

"Now let's see how well you ride

without stirrups," said Meg.

Ellie was horrified. No one had ever asked her to do that before. "I can't," she said. "I'll fall off."

"No, you won't," said Meg. She helped Ellie cross her stirrups over the front of the saddle so they were out of the way. "Now off you go. It's not as hard as you think."

Ellie squeezed nervously with her legs and Sundance walked forward. Perhaps Meg was right. It felt strange riding without stirrups but it wasn't difficult.

"Now trot on," called Meg.

Trotting was much harder. Ellie bumped and bounced so much in the saddle that she had to grab Sundance's mane to steady herself. As they went round the first corner, she slipped sideways and thought she was going to slide right off. Sundance stopped before she did.

"He's worried about you," said Meg. "He's stopping because he doesn't think you're safe."

"I don't think I am either," said Ellie, as she gave the chestnut pony a grateful pat.

"You're leaning forward. That's what's causing the problem. You'll find it much easier if you sit up straight."

Ellie felt more confident knowing Sundance was trying to help. As he started to trot again, she tried hard to keep her head up and her shoulders back.

It made a big difference. She didn't bounce
nearly as much and she felt much safer.

Suddenly, she spotted a flash of green
beside the barn. There was someone there.
She turned her head to see better. But she
accidentally leaned forward at the same time

so she started
to bump around
again. She had to
stop looking to
get her balance
back. She just
had time to see
a girl peering
out from behind
the barn – a girl
who was
watching her.

Ellie was sure it was the same face she'd seen the day before. But she didn't have another chance to look until Sundance trotted back to that part of the sand school again. By then, the watcher had gone.

Chapter 7

Ellie kept a lookout for the mystery stranger as she rode back to the yard. But she didn't see anyone. "I hope that girl's gone for good," she thought. "I don't like her watching me."

She untacked Sundance without any help and brushed away the mark left by the saddle. Then she led him out to the field and turned him loose with the others.

Sundance gave a playful buck as he trotted away. Then he rolled on the grass to give his back a good scratch. When he had finished, he stood up and shook himself from nose to tail before finally settling down to graze.

"Now it's time to muck out," said Meg. She gave Ellie a wheelbarrow, a fork, a shovel and a broom, and showed her how to take the manure and dirty straw out of Sundance's stable.

Princess Ellie to the Rescue

It was a completely new experience for Ellie. She had never tried doing such a dirty job before and, at first, the smell of the sodden straw made her wrinkle her nose. But she soon got used to it and worked her way slowly and carefully across the stable. When she had stacked all the clean bedding in a heap at the back, she swept the floor so everything looked neat and tidy. Then, feeling very pleased with herself, she set off to the muck heap with her barrow piled high with wet, dirty straw.

When she arrived, she realized she had to push it right to the top before she could empty it. There were some planks of wood to push the barrow along but it was still hard to make it go up such a steep slope. Her first attempt failed. The barrow just stopped halfway up and then rolled down again, pushing her with it.

"Perhaps I need more speed," she thought. She pulled the barrow back far enough to get a run up. Then she raced at the heap as fast as she could.

The barrow shot up the planks, bouncing slightly as it went. Ellie kept pushing hard until suddenly the barrow dropped off the end of the last plank. The wheel sank into the soft straw and the barrow stopped. Ellie couldn't. She bumped into the barrow which promptly tipped over sideways. She went with it, fell over the handle and landed flat on her face in the dirty straw.

Luckily, the muck heap was soft so only her pride was hurt. "Thank goodness no one saw me," she thought, as she struggled to her feet. But then she heard a sound. It was muffled, and stopped almost as soon as it had started, but she was sure it was a laugh.

Ellie looked around. Meg was still in the yard but the noise had come from the barn. There was someone in there and they were watching her. It must be that girl again! This time Ellie wasn't going to let her get away.

She ran towards the source of the sound, slipping and sliding as she came down the muck heap. As she raced through the barn door, she caught a brief glimpse of two legs disappearing through a window.

By the time she reached the window and looked out, there was no one to be seen. The watcher had disappeared again, but this time she'd left something behind. There was a piece of green cloth caught on a nail that stuck out of the wood.

Ellie pulled it off and looked at it. Whoever had been watching her had been wearing a green fleece. And now they were wearing a fleece with a hole.

Ellie wondered if she should tell anyone what she'd seen. But she decided not to. It was only a girl – a girl who had no right to be there. "This is my place and they're my ponies," thought Ellie. "I can handle this myself."

She pushed the scrap of material into the pocket of her jodhpurs and went back to help Meg.

Chapter 8

That night the weather changed. High winds brought dark clouds rolling in from the west and heavy rain lashed at the palace windows. In the morning, the noise of the storm made Ellie wake earlier than usual. She lay in bed wishing she could spend all day at the stables again. But she couldn't. She had to go with her parents to visit Great

Aunt Edwina who lived in a completely boring country house with no animals, no games and no TV.

Ellie knew she could ride when she got back, but that seemed such a long time away. She wanted to see her ponies before that. So she got out of bed, slipped into her riding clothes and crept downstairs.

She opened the side door quietly, pulled up the hood on her waxed jacket and ran across to the stable yard. Gipsy put his head over his door when he heard Ellie's footsteps. He looked as if he had only just woken up. There were strands of straw caught in his mane from where he'd been lying down.

Ellie stroked the grey horse and looked across at the ponies' stables. It was only

then she realized something was wrong.
Sundance's door was wide open.

She raced across the rain-soaked yard and
looked inside. But she was too late. The stable
was empty. Sundance had disappeared.

Princess Ellie to the Rescue

For a moment, Ellie was so shocked that she couldn't think what to do. Then she rushed back to the palace, calling for help.

Her shouts echoed through the building. Doors flew open in response and soon she was surrounded by maids, cleaners and secretaries, all asking what was wrong.

"Out of my way," shouted the King, as he pushed his way through the crowd. When he reached Ellie, he kneeled down and hugged her. "What on earth's happened?" he asked, gently.

"It's Sundance," sobbed Ellie. "He's gone."

"Call security! Call out the guard!" shouted the Queen, who had just rushed up in her red velvet dressing gown and silk pyjamas. Her everyday crown was perched precariously on top of her curlers.

The Pony-Mad Princess

Ellie led her parents down to the yard to show them the empty stable. The maids came with them carrying huge umbrellas to protect everyone from the pouring rain.

Meg was waiting for them. She looked as upset as Ellie felt. "I checked the stables just before I went to bed," she said. "He was definitely there then."

"He must have been stolen," said the Queen. "Whoever could have done such a dreadful thing?"

The King looked around carefully, as if he was searching for clues. "There's no sign that they went anywhere else. It looks as if they knew where Sundance would be." He paused and rubbed his chin thoughtfully. "That's strange," he said in a puzzled voice. "It must be someone who's been to the stables before."

Princess Ellie to the Rescue

His words sent a shiver down Ellie's spine as she remembered the mysterious stranger. "There's been a girl hanging around," she said. "I've seen her watching me and Sundance."

Everyone stared at her in horror.

"You silly child," shouted the King. "You should have told us."

Ellie burst into tears. "I wish I had," she sobbed. "I'm really sorry. I thought I could handle it. I never dreamed she'd do anything awful like this." She sniffed loudly and wiped away the tears with her hand in a most unprincesslike fashion.

The Pony-Mad Princess

The Queen swiftly passed her a lace-trimmed handkerchief. "Well, at least you've told us now," she said, calmly.

Suddenly there was a commotion on the other side of the yard. A soldier came in leading a girl by the arm. "I found her outside," he said. "She insists she wants to talk to the Princess."

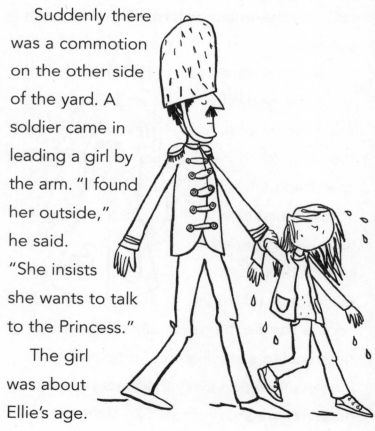

The girl was about Ellie's age.

Princess Ellie to the Rescue

She was soaking wet and her long, straight hair was matted to her head. The zip on her waxed jacket was undone. Underneath it she was wearing a green fleece – a fleece with a familiar-shaped hole.

"She's the thief!" yelled Ellie. She pulled the scrap of green material from her pocket and held it up to show it was a perfect match.

"I'm not!" shouted the girl as she pulled her arm free of the soldier's grasp. "I'm Kate. I'm staying with my grandparents. My gran's the palace cook."

Ellie stared at her suspiciously. "So why were you watching me?" she asked.

For the first time, Kate looked slightly guilty. "Gran told me not to bother you," she said. "But I love horses so much I just wanted to be near them."

The Queen stepped forward and pointed at her accusingly. "Is that why you stole Princess Aurelia's pony?" she asked.

"I didn't take him," said Kate. "No one did. He got out by himself."

"Rubbish," said the King. "Horses can't open doors."

"Some of them can," said Meg, thoughtfully. She closed the stable door and tested the bolt. It slid backwards and forwards easily. "Maybe Sundance has only just learned."

Kate rushed over and grabbed Ellie by the hands. "You've got to believe me," she pleaded. "I came to see the ponies really early before anyone was up. I saw Sundance undo the bolt with his tongue and run off, so I followed him. I thought I could catch him and bring him back. But he's fallen in a ditch and he can't get out."

Ellie felt her stomach knot with fear. She couldn't bear it if anything happened to Sundance. "What are we going to do?" she asked. "We've got to save him."

"We'll send out a rescue team," said her father. He listened carefully while Kate described the exact position of the ditch. Then he shook his head. "It'll take a long time to get heavy lifting gear out there."

Ellie imagined how frightened Sundance must be. "We can't leave him on his own," she said. "I'll run on ahead and keep him calm."

"But princesses don't..." began her father, stepping in front of her to block her path.

"This one does," said Ellie, as she ducked past him and ran off into the driving rain.

Kate ran after her. "You'll get there quicker if I show you the way."

Princess Ellie to the Rescue

Behind them, Ellie could hear voices shouting "Come back" and "Be careful" but she didn't care. All that mattered was keeping Sundance safe.

Chapter 9

Ellie and Kate ran side by side up the lane and across the park to the stream. Normally this was a gentle, babbling brook. But the rain had swollen it into a torrent. As their feet pounded across the wooden bridge, Ellie glanced over the side at the deep, fast-flowing water. She felt a shiver of fear. The rain would be filling the ditch as well.

Princess Ellie to the Rescue

"This way," said Kate when they reached the other side. She led them up a slope and then turned right into the wood.

To Ellie's relief, the trees gave them a little shelter from the wind and rain. She was already soaking wet and she was tired too. Running so far and so fast was hard work and she wasn't used to it. But she couldn't stop now. Sundance needed her.

They ran through the wood, twisting and turning between the trees until they came to a large area of sloping ground.

"Sundance is down there," said Kate.

It was difficult to run down the hill. Their feet slithered and slipped on the wet grass. But they didn't stop until they reached the ditch where Sundance was trapped. It was deeper than Ellie had expected. Its sides were steep and muddy. Large grooves showed where Sundance's hooves had slid in the slippery mud as he had tried unsuccessfully to climb out.

Ellie's eyes filled with tears when she saw the chestnut pony. He was completely exhausted by his efforts to escape, and was lying on his side in the shallow water at the bottom of the ditch. Luckily, his head was resting a little way up the bank, just clear of the surface, so he could still breathe.

"Sundance, Sundance," Ellie called. "We're here and there's help on the way."

Princess Ellie to the Rescue

The pony lifted his head slightly when
he heard her voice, and whickered gently.
Then his head fell back onto the bank
and he lay still.

"He's too tired and weak to save himself,"
said Ellie. "He can't even stand up."

Kate nodded. "That's not the only
problem. There's much more water in the
ditch than when I left."

"And it's still raining," said Ellie with
alarm. "If the level keeps going up, his head
will be under the water and he'll drown."

"I hope the rescue party gets here soon,"
said Kate, nervously.

"So do I," said Ellie. "But we can't let
him die. It's up to us to keep him safe
until they arrive."

They slithered down the slippery bank

to where Sundance lay. Ellie gently stroked his nose and the pony flicked his ears slightly in response. "He's so cold and wet," she said. "We've got to do something to warm him up."

She took off her jacket and laid it over the part of his body that was still clear of the water. Kate put hers over him too and they both shivered as the rain soaked quickly through their fleeces.

Princess Ellie to the Rescue

"If we're colder, he must be warmer," said Kate.

Ellie had another idea. "I read in one of my pony books that a horse feels warmer if his ears are warm," she said. So they crouched down and rubbed his cold, wet ears, trying to warm them in their hands.

The rain continued to pour down and the water in the ditch rose higher and higher. Soon it lapped at Sundance's nose. The pony made a feeble effort to lift it clear. Then his head dropped back.

Ellie sat down in the mud and lifted his head onto her lap. Her legs were in the water now. It was freezing cold, but at least Sundance was safe for a little longer.

Kate sat down beside her. "Let's talk," she said as they huddled together for warmth. "It'll take our minds off how cold and wet we are."

Ellie stroked Sundance's head and concentrated on Kate's voice as she described how her dad's job took him and her mum all over the world. She'd gone with them when she was small. Now she was older, she was staying with her gran and grandad so she didn't have to keep changing schools.

Princess Ellie to the Rescue

When Kate stopped, Ellie's mind immediately snapped back to the present. She realized with a shudder that the water had risen even higher. She didn't want to think what would happen if the others didn't get here soon. "Let's keep talking," she said. "It's my turn now."

She had just started describing a waving lesson when she heard a shout. She looked over her shoulder and saw Meg, her father and several other people waving at them. The rescue party had arrived. But were they in time to save Sundance?

Chapter 10

Meg slithered down the bank towards them. She was holding a wide canvas strap with a ring at each end. "We've got to put this around Sundance's tummy so we can pull him free."

Ellie held Sundance's head safely on her lap while Meg and Kate waded into the water, struggling to get the strap in position. It would have been impossible if he'd been lying on hard ground. But the mud which had trapped the pony was just soft enough to let them slowly wiggle the strap underneath him.

As soon as it was in place, the men on the bank let down a long rope with a hook on the end. Meg grabbed it and clipped it onto the rings. "We're ready," she shouted.

Ellie heard the roar of a tractor's engine and saw the rope pull tight. The strap around Sundance tightened too. The pony felt it and started to panic. Summoning the last of his energy, he started to thrash his legs wildly to escape the strap.

Ellie stroked his head. "Steady, boy," she said. "Stay still. It'll all be over soon."

Sundance flicked his ears towards her voice and grew calmer.

"Keep going," said Meg. "He likes the sound of your voice."

So Ellie kept talking. She told him how beautiful he was and how much she loved him. She talked about the warm stable waiting for him and the wonderful rides they would have together. And Sundance listened to her and lay still while the tractor pulled him slowly up the bank to safety.

As soon as he was out of the ditch, everyone rushed to help him. Meg started to rub him dry with handfuls of straw. The tractor driver put some blankets over him, and the vet listened to his heart with a stethoscope.

Ellie and Kate watched anxiously as they stood shivering in the rain. At last, the vet straightened up and smiled at them. "He's going to be fine," he said. "He just needs to get warm and have a good, long rest."

The two girls sighed with relief. Then Ellie grabbed some straw and went to help Meg. But the King took hold of her arm and stopped her.

"You've done enough already," he said. "You were naughty to run off like that, but you saved Sundance's life. Now you both need to get dry and warm yourselves."

"But I can't leave him now," said Ellie through chattering teeth.

"Your mother guessed that," he said with a laugh. "That's why she's put dry clothes and towels in the back of the Range Rover." He turned to Kate and added, "There's some for you too. And your grandmother insisted on packing hot chocolate and cream buns."

It was lovely to climb into the car, away from the wind and rain. Ellie and Kate peeled off their wet clothes and wrapped themselves in thick fleecy towels. They rubbed their arms and legs hard to bring back some warmth into them and, as soon as they were dry, they pulled on their clean clothes.

Kate found the flask and poured out the

Princess Ellie to the Rescue

hot chocolate.
They sat together
warming their
hands on the
hot mugs while
they watched
the rescuers
helping
Sundance.
He was starting
to move now.
He lifted his head

to look around. Then, with a huge effort,
he heaved himself to his feet.

The girls joined in the cheers and watched
Meg lead him into the trailer behind the Range
Rover. Then they ate the buns to celebrate, as
she drove them back to the stable yard.

When they arrived, Meg lowered the ramp on the trailer, but she didn't go in. "You lead him out," she said to Ellie. "He's your pony."

Ellie ran into the trailer and untied Sundance. As she led him to the top of the ramp, she saw Kate looking at her. Ellie paused for a moment as memories of the last few days raced through her brain – the face in the woods, running through the rain, and huddling together in the ditch with Sundance. Then she made up her mind, took a deep breath and said, "I don't want you watching me any more."

Kate looked embarrassed and stared at her feet. "I won't," she muttered. "I promise." She turned to go.

"Don't be silly," yelled Ellie. "I don't

want you watching me because I want you to *ride* with me."

Kate turned back quickly. Her face lit up with a huge smile. "Brilliant," she said.

"Come and help then," said Ellie, with a laugh.

Together, they led Sundance down the ramp and into the waiting stable. Princess Ellie felt blissfully happy. At last, she had a friend to share her ponies with.

Pony-Mad Fun & Facts

Dear Reader,

Are you as pony-mad as Princess Ellie? I am. I've loved ponies for as long as I can remember. But I didn't get the pony I dreamed of until I was grown up.

When I was a child, I had to make do with reading about ponies and making up imaginary stories about them. Maybe that's why I write pony books now.

I hope you enjoy Princess Ellie's adventures and, because I remember how much I loved learning about ponies, there are some fantastic facts and fun quiz questions just for you in the following pages...

Love,

x x

Meet Princess Ellie's ponies

Sundance

You've read all about how
Sundance got lost in the wood –
now find out a little bit more about him...

COLOUR: Chestnut with a white mark
on the front of his face called a blaze

LIKES: Shadow

DISLIKES: Things that startle him

ABOUT SUNDANCE: Sundance is a real
schoolmaster. He's very trustworthy and
reliable, although he can spook sometimes
if he's frightened.

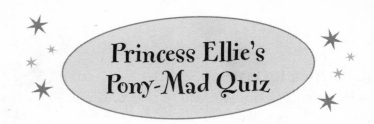

Princess Ellie's Pony-Mad Quiz

Do you know your **riding hat** from your **reins**? Do you know what colour **Sundance** is? Test your knowledge of Princess Ellie's world with this quiz!

1. Princess Ellie's new palace groom is called:
a) Meg
b) Miss Stringle
c) Shadow

2. Which of Ellie's horses can open the stable door with his tongue?
a) Shadow
b) Sundance
c) Moonbeam

3. To get all the dirt out of her horses' hooves, Ellie has to use a:
a) Hoof pick
b) Hairbrush
c) Pencil

4. Tacking up is:
a) Putting on a horse's saddle and bridle
b) Putting up a poster
c) Speeding up when a horse is cantering

5. Sundance is a:
a) Black Shetland pony
b) Grey Welsh pony
c) Chestnut pony with a white blaze

6. What vehicle is used to transport Sundance home?
a) Bicycle
b) Trailer
c) Caravan

7. The "bit" is part of a pony's bridle, and it goes in the pony's:
a) Ears
b) Mouth
c) Eyes

Turn the page to
find out the answers...

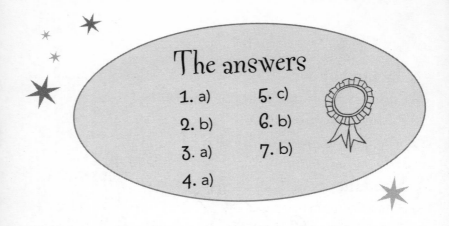

The answers

1. a)   5. c)

2. b)   6. b)

3. a)   7. b)

4. a)

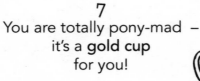
Tot up your total to see just how pony-mad you are...

1-3
A good try.

4-6
Great knowledge and a big rosette!

7
You are totally pony-mad –
it's a **gold cup**
for you!

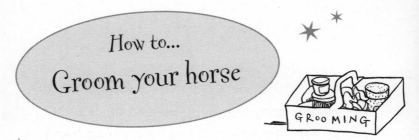

How to...
Groom your horse

Princess Ellie loves grooming her ponies, and can spend hours in the stables. Here are her top tips for great grooming:

* Never brush wet legs. You might scratch the skin underneath. Wait until any mud is dry before you try to brush it off.

* Be careful when brushing under the pony's tummy. Some ponies are ticklish.

* Use a soft brush on manes and tails. Stiff brushes and combs can snap the long hairs.

* When you're brushing the tail, it's safer to stand beside the pony's hind leg instead of directly behind him. Hold all the long hairs in one hand and brush out a few at a time with the other hand.

* Use a hoof pick to clean all the dirt out of the pony's hooves, but be careful not to hurt the soft triangular part that's called the frog.

* Brush on hoof oil or ointment to make the pony's feet gleam.

* Ponies who live out in a field need the oil in their coats to keep them dry, so don't brush it all out. Just brush them enough to make them look clean and tidy.

Read on for a sneak preview of
Princess Ellie's next adventure...

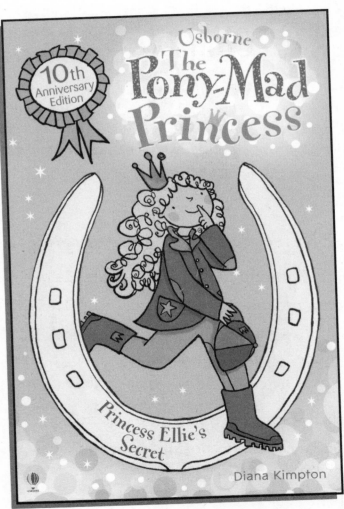

Usborne
The
Pony-Mad
Princess

10th Anniversary Edition

Princess Ellie's Secret

Diana Kimpton

Chapter 1

"Steady, Shadow," said Princess Ellie. The black Shetland pony she was riding pawed at the ground with a tiny front hoof. He was keen to start the dressing-up race, and couldn't understand the delay.

"Are you all right down there?" asked Kate, with a grin. She was riding Sundance, Ellie's chestnut pony, who was much taller than Shadow.

Ellie grinned back. "Just you wait," she said. "Sometimes it's good to be small." She was so glad Kate had come to live with her grandparents, who worked at the palace. It was good to have a friend at last, and they had so much fun together with Ellie's four ponies.

"Are you two ready?" called Meg, the palace groom. When they both nodded, she shouted, "One, two, three, GO." The two ponies leaped forward and galloped across the field towards two piles of clothes on the other side. Ellie leaned forward, urging

Shadow on. But the Shetland's short legs were no match for Sundance. Soon, the chestnut pony pulled ahead and reached Kate's pile of clothes first.

"Bother," thought Ellie, as she saw Kate leap off and start putting on a long floppy coat. Then Shadow finally reached the other pile and she had to concentrate on her own part in the race.

Jumping off was easy – her feet were nearly touching the ground anyway. Then she pulled on a long coat, wrapped a scarf around her neck and crammed a wide-brimmed hat on top of her pink and gold crash cap.

She glanced over at Kate, expecting to see her on her way back. But she wasn't. She was struggling to mount Sundance. Now she was dressed up, she was finding it hard to lift her foot high enough to reach the saddle.

"We've still got a chance, Shadow," cried Ellie. She didn't have Kate's problem. Shadow was so small that she managed to jump into the saddle without using the stirrups at all.

She urged the Shetland into a gallop and headed back towards the finishing line. Soon she could hear Sundance's hooves pounding after them, but this time the lead was too great. Shadow raced across the line just ahead of the chestnut pony.

"Ellie's the winner," shouted Meg.

"Well done," said Kate. "Being small was definitely useful that time."

Suddenly a voice called, "Princess Aurelia!"

Ellie looked round and saw Miss Stringle standing at the palace end of the field. She always insisted on using Ellie's full name. To Ellie's annoyance, so did nearly everyone else in the royal household, especially the King and Queen. Ellie trotted Shadow across the field to say hello. But as soon as she was close enough to see her governess's face, she realized something was wrong.

"Whatever are you doing, Your Royal Highness?" asked Miss Stringle, giving Ellie one of her disapproving looks.

Ellie ignored the look and cheerfully replied, "We're playing mounted games. I just won. Did you see?"

"Indeed I did," declared Miss Stringle. "And I'm horrified to see you making such an exhibition of yourself. It is not suitable behaviour for a princess."

Ellie felt confused. Surely there was nothing wrong with winning. Then she remembered the hat, coat and scarf. "I had to wear these," she explained, as she pulled off the hat. "You can't go in a dressing-up race without dressing up."

"I am not talking about the clothes," said Miss Stringle, crossly. "It's the pony that's the problem. It's much too small." As she spoke, she waved her hand at Shadow. The greedy Shetland instantly assumed he was being offered food. He stuck out his nose and nuzzled Miss Stringle's outstretched palm. She pulled her

hand away quickly and
dabbed it clean with a
lace-trimmed hankie.

Normally, Ellie would
have been tempted to
laugh. But this time, she
was too full of
indignation. "Shadow's
not too small," she said.
"He's exactly the
right size for a
Shetland."

"But that's not the
right size for *you*," said Miss
Stringle. "You look ridiculous. I'll have to
tell your parents." Without waiting for Ellie
to reply, she marched back to the palace
with a determined look on her face.

Ellie's heart sank. Deep down inside, she knew Miss Stringle was right. Shadow was her very first pony and she could hardly remember the time when he wasn't there for her to love. He'd been her best birthday present the year she was four and he'd been just the right size for her then. But over the years, she had grown and he hadn't. Now her feet nearly touched the ground when she was riding him. She had hoped no one else would notice. What would happen to Shadow if she couldn't ride him any more?

To find out what happens next read

Princess Ellie's Secret

Don't miss a single sparkling
adventure of

The
Pony-Mad
Princess

Now also
available as
ebooks

If you like The Pony-Mad Princess
you might also like

Amy Wild, Animal Talker

by Diana Kimpton

The Secret Necklace

Amy is thrilled to discover she can talk to animals!
But making friends is harder than she thought...

ISBN 9781409504290

The Musical Mouse

There's a singing mouse at Amy's school! Can Amy
find it a new home before the headmaster catches it?

ISBN 9781409504306

The Mystery Cat

Amy has to track down the owners of a playful
ginger cat who's lost his home...and his memory.

ISBN 9781409504313

The Furry Detectives

Things have been going missing on the Island and
Amy suspects there's a thief at work.

ISBN 9781409504320

The Great Sheep Race

Will Amy train the Island's sheep in time for her
school fair's big fundraiser – a Great Sheep Race?

ISBN 9781409504337

The Star-Struck Parrot

Amy gets to be an extra in a film shot on the Island...
but can she land Plato the parrot a part too?

ISBN 9781409504344

The Lost Treasure

An ancient ring is discovered on the Island, sparking a
hunt for buried treasure...and causing chaos.

ISBN 9781409521037

The Vanishing Cat

When one of the animals in the clan goes missing,
Amy faces her biggest mystery yet...

ISBN 9781409521044

Check out more sparkly stories at
www.usborne.com/fiction